A Spy in the White House

by **Ron Roy**
illustrated by **Timothy Bush**

A STEPPING STONE BOOK™

Random House 🏠 New York

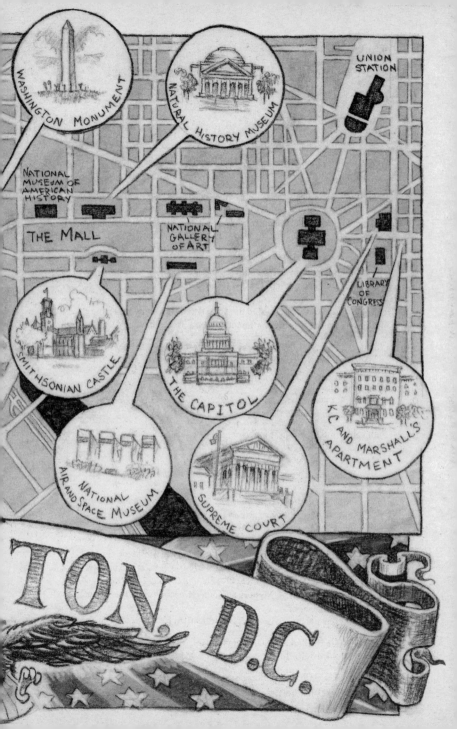

This is for Cabby, super cat.

—R.R.

Photo credits: p. 88, top, and p. 89, courtesy of the Library of Congress; p. 88, bottom, Cecil Stoughton, White House/John Fitzgerald Kennedy Library, Boston.

Visit us on the Web!
www.steppingstonesbooks.com
www.randomhouse.com/kids

Educators and librarians, for a variety of teaching tools, visit us at
www.randomhouse.com/teachers

Library of Congress Cataloging-in-Publication Data
Roy, Ron.
A spy in the White House / by Ron Roy ; illustrated by Timothy Bush.
    p.   cm. — (Capital mysteries ; #4)
"A Stepping Stone Book."
Summary: KC tries to uncover the White House spy who is leaking secrets about the upcoming wedding of her mother and the president.
ISBN 978-0-375-82557-6 (pbk.) — ISBN 978-0-375-92557-3 (lib. bdg.)
[1. White House (Washington, D.C.)—Fiction. 2. Spies—Fiction.
3. Weddings—Fiction. 4. Mystery and detective stories.] I. Bush, Timothy,
ill. II. Title. III. Series.
PZ7.R8139Sp 2004   [E]—dc22   2003015110

Printed in the United States of America
20 19 18 17 16 15 14

Contents

1
Who's Listening?

"Come on down, George Washington. It's time to go outside," KC said.

The president's cat, George, was sitting on top of the refrigerator.

"Will you get him down, Marshall?" KC asked. "We have to practice for the wedding."

KC Corcoran and Marshall Li were best friends. They lived in Washington, D.C. But today, they were in the White House. KC's mom was going to marry the President of the United States next week!

KC would hold her mom's flowers during the ceremony, and Marshall would be the ring bearer—with George's help.

"What's to practice?" Marshall grumbled. "Your mom says 'I do,' then the president says 'I do,' then it's over."

KC rolled her eyes. "This is a White House wedding, Marsh," she said. "Everything has to be perfect. The whole world will be watching on TV!"

Marshall raised his eyebrows. "I'll be on TV?" he asked.

KC nodded. "We'll all be on TV," she said. "Even George. That's why we have to practice making him walk down the aisle."

Marshall grabbed George while KC opened the door that led out of the president's private quarters.

Arnold, the marine guard on duty, saluted them. "Afternoon, KC," he said. "Afternoon, Marshall."

"Hi, Arnold," the kids said.

Arnold took off one white glove and stroked George under the chin. Then he sneezed.

"Are you allergic to cats?" Marshall asked.

Arnold sniffed. "No, I have a cold and a sore throat," he said with a hoarse voice. KC noticed that Arnold's nose was red. His eyes looked watery and puffy.

"I hope you feel better for the wedding," KC said.

"Thanks," Arnold said. "I'll try."

KC and Marshall left Arnold and walked to the rose garden. Marshall set George down, and KC tied a green ribbon to his collar.

"Why does George need a silly green ribbon?" Marshall asked. "What's wrong

3

with a piece of rope or something?"

"The ribbon matches Mom's dress, my dress, and your vest," KC reminded him. "The wedding is color-coordinated!"

"Maybe I'll get sick like Arnold," Marshall muttered. He looked at his hand. "You know, my skin does look a little green."

"Perfect, you'll fit right into the color scheme!" KC crowed. "Let's get started."

KC pulled a wad of string from her pocket and made a long, straight line on the lawn. "This is where we have to walk," she said to Marshall. "The wedding guests will be sitting in chairs on both sides."

"*I* know that," said Marshall. "But someone had better explain it to George."

George was half under a bush, investigating a line of ants.

"Get him out of there before his ribbon gets tangled," KC said.

Marshall tugged George out from under the bush and set him down near the string.

"Okay!" KC began humming the wedding march. She took small steps over to where the president would be waiting.

"Now it's time for the rings," KC called to Marshall.

"Come on, George, let's walk," said Marshall as he bent to pick up the cat's ribbon. But George had a different idea. He bolted across the lawn, the ribbon flying behind him.

"Hey, that's the wrong way!" Marshall yelled. He and KC chased after George, who disappeared in some shrubbery.

"Marsh, why'd you let him run away?"

KC asked. She peeked into a thorny bush covered with pink rose blossoms.

"I didn't *let* him do anything!" Marshall said. "I'm not an animal trainer, you know."

"I hope he doesn't take off during the wedding," KC said. "He'll have the wedding rings around his neck."

"That's why we're practicing," Marshall said. "And so far it's a big flop!"

The kids searched under all the rose-bushes. No George.

They crawled on their hands and knees and peeked under the hedges. George stayed out of sight.

They looked up in the tall trees that lined the fences surrounding the White House. They saw birds and squirrels, but no large, fluffy cat with a green ribbon tied to his collar.

Twenty minutes later, they still hadn't found George. They had searched most of the grounds around the White House.

"Should we check outside the fence?" Marshall asked. "Maybe he snuck under."

"I know!" KC said. She dug a bag of Kitty Kandy out of her pocket and started shaking it.

Traffic whizzed by on Pennsylvania Avenue. Horns honked, brakes squealed, and a motorcycle roared past.

"George will never hear you rattling that stuff," Marshall said.

Just then George walked out of the hedges. KC gave Marshall a look.

Marshall ignored her and picked up George. "Bad cat!" he said. "You could get smushed out there!"

KC gave George a treat and put the

bag back in her pocket. "That's weird. George smells like mint. I think he's been in the herb garden," she told Marshall.

Marshall rolled his eyes. "You're just imagining another mystery," he teased.

KC checked her watch. "Well, there's one thing I'm not imagining. We've got to go! The press conference is starting!"

"Can't we skip it?" Marshall asked. "Let's go to Rock Creek Park and look for bugs!"

"We can go to the park anytime," KC said. "But how often does my mom marry the president?"

"You really want to see all those reporters," Marshall said.

"I can't help it," KC said. "Someday when I'm a big Washington reporter, maybe I'll interview you!"

She and Marshall hurried to the Oval Office. When they burst through the door, they saw about twenty reporters waving their hands and aiming microphones toward the president.

KC's mom and the president were sitting side by side on a long white sofa. Lois smiled at KC and patted the seat next to hers.

KC sat down by her mom. George jumped out of Marshall's arms and hopped onto President Thornton's lap.

KC felt embarrassed when everyone stared at her. Her mother took her hand and squeezed it.

Marshall watched from the back of the room. For the next fifteen minutes, the president and Lois answered a lot of questions. Everyone wanted to know how they met. Everyone wanted to know about the wedding and who would be invited.

Then one female reporter asked the president where he and Lois were going on their honeymoon.

"We're keeping that information in the family," the president said, smiling as the cameras clicked away.

"Ms. Corcoran, can you tell us about your wedding dress?" the woman asked. "What does it look like? Who designed it for you?"

KC had seen her mother's pale green dress. It was hanging in a closet upstairs in the White House. KC thought it was the most gorgeous dress in the world. She couldn't wait to see her mother wear it on her wedding day.

"That's going to be a surprise for the

wedding," Lois said. "But I can tell you this much—it's beautiful!"

The president set George on the floor and stood up. "I'm afraid that has to be the last question," he said. "Lois and I have a lot of plans to make. Thank you all for coming!"

The reporters gathered their stuff and filed out of the room.

"Well, that wasn't so bad, was it?" the president asked when all the press had gone.

"Why didn't you say where you're going on your honeymoon?" Marshall asked.

"We don't want a thousand reporters and helicopters buzzing around," the president said. He took Lois by the hand. "Now let's go find out what's for lunch."

The next morning, KC, her mom, and

Marshall arrived at the White House to have breakfast with the president. They found him in his dining room, staring at the newspaper.

"You're not going to believe this," the president said. He turned the paper so they could all see.

Covering almost the whole front page was a picture of the Island Paradise Hotel in Maui, Hawaii. Beneath the picture were these words:

PRESIDENT AND BRIDE TO HONEYMOON IN HAWAIIAN ISLAND HOTEL

2

There's a Spy in the White House

"How did they find out?" KC asked.

"I wish I knew," the president said grimly. "They even found the hotel on Maui."

He glanced at Lois, KC, and Marshall. "I don't suppose any of you accidentally let the cat out of the bag?"

"I certainly didn't," Lois said. "I want our honeymoon to be private."

"I didn't either," said KC.

They all looked at Marshall.

"I know how to keep a secret!" cried Marshall. "Besides, I didn't know the name of the hotel."

"Well, someone found out, and they told Darla Darling," Lois said.

Darla Darling wrote the society column for the *Star* newspaper. Her picture was at the top of her column.

"I saw her at the press conference yesterday," Marshall told them.

"Yes, she was the reporter who asked about the honeymoon and my dress," Lois said.

"Maybe someone at the hotel blabbed to her," Marshall suggested.

The president shook his head. "The hotel people in Hawaii didn't know our real names," he said. "Lois and I were registered as Mr. and Mrs. Smith."

"Well, I'm going to get to the bottom of this," Lois said. She picked up a telephone and called the newspaper. She asked to speak to Darla Darling. A few seconds later, she hung up.

"Her voice mail," Lois explained. "'Ms. Darling is on assignment and not available.'"

The president picked up a different telephone and asked Vice President Mary Kincaid to come in. When she arrived, the president showed her the newspaper.

"How did Darla Darling find out?" the vice president asked. "That was top-secret information!"

"None of us leaked it," the president said. "Could it have been someone on my staff?"

"I can't imagine that," Mary said. "They knew you and Lois wanted your honeymoon spot kept a secret."

"Secret or not, Darla Darling found

out," Lois said. "And she didn't hear it from some little bird!"

"No, but it could have been a little bug," Marshall said.

Everyone looked at him.

"What do you mean, Marshall?" the president asked.

Marshall pointed to the flower vase on the table. "Someone could have planted a bug!" he whispered.

KC gasped. "Do you think?" She got up and walked around the room, peering into small spaces.

"It's not likely that anyone could have gotten a listening device in here," the president said. "These rooms are very secure."

"Marshall may have a point. I'll have the place swept just to be sure," Mary

Kincaid said. "Meanwhile, will you two be choosing a different place for your honeymoon?"

"Definitely," the president said. He looked across the table at Lois. "How about—"

"Shhh," Lois whispered, grinning. "The walls may have ears. We'll talk about it later."

"At least Darla Darling didn't find out about your dress," KC said to her mother.

Lois smiled. "It's the most beautiful dress in the world," she said. "Michael is a genius!"

During the night, the FBI checked the president's private residence for bugs. They found nothing.

The next morning, a drawing of Lois's wedding dress took up almost all of Darla

Darling's column in the newspaper. There was even a picture of Michael, the man who had designed the dress. The headline over the picture read:

NEW FIRST LADY'S DRESS IS GRAND, GREEN, AND GORGEOUS!

3

The Stranger's Voice

KC dashed into her mother's bedroom with the newspaper. Lois was still asleep, but not for long.

"Mom, wake up! Look at this!"

Lois rolled over and blinked at her excited daughter. Then she looked at the clock. "Honey, it's only seven o'clock. What's so important?"

"I went downstairs to get the paper. Look!" KC held the newspaper in front of her mother. "They found out about your dress!"

Lois looked at the pictures and read the headline. "Oh my goodness," she whispered. Then she reached for the telephone and called the president.

While her mom showered and dressed, KC called Marshall. He lived in her apartment building, two floors down. The phone rang five times before KC heard someone pick up.

"Niagara Falls, drop over," Marshall's sleepy voice said into KC's ear.

"Have you seen today's newspaper?" KC nearly shouted.

"I'm still in bed, KC," Marshall said. "All I see is my pillow."

"You're not going to believe it," KC said. "Get dressed and meet us in the lobby in fifteen minutes!"

A half hour later, KC, her mom, and Marshall met the president in his private White House rooms. He was sitting at the table in the little kitchen. His hair was messed up and he hadn't shaved. The newspaper was spread out on the table. Yvonne, the president's private maid, set bagels, glasses, and a pitcher of orange juice on the counter, then left the room.

"This is so creepy!" Marshall said, staring at the newspaper. "How did they find out?"

"This drawing of my dress isn't exactly right," Lois muttered. "But it's close enough. And the only people who knew what the dress looked like were the four of us, the vice president, and Michael."

"Maybe Michael told Darla," KC suggested.

Lois shook her head. "No. Michael never talks about his clients. He has to keep secrets, or he wouldn't last long in the dress-designing business. Besides, I never told him where we were going on our honeymoon."

"How about the people who work for him?" the president asked.

"Only Michael knew who the dress was really for," Lois said. "I told him to write L. Smith on the order."

Marshall got himself a bagel and dropped a small piece on the floor. George leaped from the refrigerator to the counter, then to the floor. He pounced on the morsel and carried it to a corner.

"I don't understand it," KC said. "How could someone be listening? Didn't the FBI check for bugs last night?"

"Yes, they gave this place a thorough going-over," the president said.

Lois sighed. "Well, I wanted to keep

my wedding dress a secret, but now the world knows."

"I'm sorry about your dress," the president said. "But if someone has managed to learn our wedding secrets, they might also be overhearing other things we talk about." He glanced around the table. "Like national security."

Marshall's eyes widened. "You mean top-secret information?"

"That's exactly what I mean," President Thornton said. He glanced at Lois. "Maybe we should postpone the wedding till we clear this up."

"You can't cancel the wedding!" KC cried.

"Oh, we'll still get married," the president said. "But maybe we should put it off till we find out what's going on."

"Zachary is right," KC's mom said. "We can hardly go on our honeymoon if there's a spy in the White House!"

"I'll get to the bottom of this mystery," the president said. "Right now, I'm going to get the FBI back in here for another bug check!"

"And I'm going to call the hotel in Hawaii and tell them the Smiths have changed their mind," Lois said. "Then I'll think about a different dress."

The president and KC's mom left the room with George tagging along behind them.

"Come on," KC told Marshall. "I have an idea."

"I do, too," Marshall said, following KC past Arnold and into the hallway. "I want to go to Rock Creek Park. The bugs will just be coming out to sun themselves on the rocks."

"I promise we'll go to the park, just not right now," KC said. "Don't you want to figure out who's spying on my mom and the president?"

"Okay, what's your idea?" Marshall asked as he and KC left the White House.

"We're going to see Darla Darling," KC said.

"That society lady?" Marshall yelped. "Oh, great. Just what I need. She'll probably make us drink tea out of itty-bitty cups. I'll be bored to death!"

"Marsh, Darla Darling started this whole thing," KC said. "She may be the link to whoever is spying on the White House!"

KC and Marshall kept walking along

Pennsylvania Avenue until they reached the offices of the *Star* newspaper. Opposite the front door was a big desk. A woman with blond hair sat there typing at a keyboard. Through a doorway on the right, KC could see people working at computers and talking on telephones. A doorway on the left opened on a long, empty hallway.

The woman with blond hair looked up. "May I help you?" she asked.

"We're here to see Darla Darling," KC said.

The woman squinted at KC. "Do you have an appointment?" she asked. "Ms. Darling is very busy."

"I'm KC Corcoran. My mom is marrying the president," KC said.

The woman's eyes widened. She

reached for her telephone and dialed. "Hello, Darla, there's a Miss Corcoran here to see you. No, not Lois Corcoran. It's her daughter."

Five seconds later, KC and Marshall heard footsteps tapping down the hallway. A tall woman with broad shoulders was striding toward them. She wore a black pants suit and black high-heeled boots. Her dark, curly hair bounced when she walked.

"Hello, I'm Darla Darling," the woman said in a smooth, low voice. Her blue eyes gleamed like wet marbles.

KC had to tilt her head back to see the woman's face. "I'm KC, and this is my friend Marshall," KC said. "We want to talk to you about my mom's wedding."

"Wonderful!" Darla said. "Follow me."

She spun around and strode back down the hallway. KC and Marshall had to practically run to keep up.

At the end of the hall, Darla Darling entered an open doorway. She sat in a swivel chair behind a messy desk. "Have a seat," she said, waving a hand at a pair of purple chairs.

The kids sat. KC glanced around the cluttered office. She saw a computer, a fax machine, two telephones, a tape recorder, a small TV set, and a bunch of other stuff. Papers were scattered across the desk.

Along one wall was a small bed. It was neatly made up with pillows and a bright red cover. Next to the bed were a sink and mirror. Lined up on the sink counter were a toothbrush and toothpaste, a bottle of green mouthwash, and lots of small jars.

Cool, thought KC. *She's so busy she even sleeps here. Someday when I'm a reporter, I'll do that, too!*

Darla Darling flipped open a pad and picked up a pencil. "So, what did you want to tell me?" she asked KC and Marshall.

KC gulped. "I really wanted to ask you something," she said.

Darla Darling leaned forward. "I'm listening."

"How did you find out about my mom's dress and where she was going on her honeymoon?" KC asked.

Ms. Darling's eyes opened wide. "Surely you don't expect me to tell you that?" she asked, smiling. Her teeth were big and white.

"That stuff was a secret," Marshall said. "No one is supposed to know."

Darla shrugged her wide shoulders. "My job is to report the news to my readers," she said. "And when the president gets married, *that's* news!"

"But their honeymoon and Mom's dress were private!" KC said. "The president wants to know how you found out!"

Darla Darling sighed. "All right. Someone telephoned me with the information. I don't know who it was, and even if I did, I wouldn't tell you."

She tapped one of the phones with her pencil. "If I revealed my sources, this phone would stop ringing. I'd be out of business just like that," she said, snapping her fingers.

Darla stood up and walked toward the door. "Now if you'll excuse me, I have a thousand things to do."

KC and Marshall followed her to the door.

"Isn't there anything you can tell us about who called you?" asked KC. "The president really wants to know."

Darla Darling looked down at the two kids. She closed her eyes as if she were trying to remember. Then she smiled.

"Well, I do remember one thing," she said. "The caller had a scratchy voice."

4
Two Suspects

KC and Marshall left the *Star* offices and headed back to the White House.

"That was a waste of time," Marshall said. "We didn't learn anything."

"Yes, we did," KC said. "We know how Darla Darling gets her information."

"But we don't know who's calling her," said Marshall.

"Right, but we do know it's someone with a scratchy voice," said KC.

"How does that help?" Marshall asked. "On TV, spies always try to disguise their voice. This guy probably sounded that way on purpose."

"Okay, you're right," KC said. "But we do know something else. The caller has to be someone close to the president."

"Hey, wait a minute!" Marshall cried. "How about Arnold? He's always standing outside the president's door! And he's got a cold, so his voice is hoarse!"

"Arnold?" KC stopped walking. "Yeah, he could have overheard Mom and the president talking! But why would he tell Darla Darling?"

"For money!" Marshall said. "Maybe she pays him for information."

"But she told us she doesn't know who the caller is," KC said. "How could she pay him?"

Marshall thought for a minute. "Maybe Arnold tells her where to leave the money, then he goes and gets it later. Darla wouldn't have to know who she was leaving the money for."

The kids kept walking. Soon they were at the White House. They walked to the rear parking lot. The private entrance was near some hedges.

"Look, there's the vice president," KC said to Marshall. "What's she doing?"

They watched Vice President Kincaid. She had her hand cupped over her mouth and was speaking into a cell phone. She kept glancing around, as if she didn't want to be overheard. KC tried to eavesdrop, but she was too far away.

The vice president snapped her phone shut, crossed the lot, and disappeared into the White House.

KC stared at the spot where the vice president had been standing. "You know,

Arnold isn't the only one who's always near the president's door," she said after a minute. "The vice president walks in and out all the time."

"Ms. Kincaid? Why would she spy on the president?" Marshall asked. "I don't think she needs the money."

"I don't know, but Mom showed her the dress a few days ago," KC said. "And the president must have told her where they were going on their honeymoon. Let's keep an eye on her."

The kids entered the White House through the private door. Arnold was stationed outside the president's private rooms.

He sneezed and blew his nose. "Hi, kids," he said.

"How's your cold?" KC asked.

Arnold grinned and stuffed his handkerchief into a pocket. "I think it's getting better," he said.

KC listened to his raspy voice. "Do you know anyone named Darla?" she asked.

"I don't think so. I know a Dora and a Denise, and my sister's name is Debi," he said. "But no Darlas."

He took out a box of lozenges and put one on his tongue. "Want one?" he asked. "They're cough drops, but they taste pretty good. They're called Minti-Meds. I take 'em for my sore throat." Arnold held out the box as he opened the door.

"No thanks," KC said.

When KC and Marshall walked into the president's rooms, they got a shock. KC's mom was crying. The president stood next to her, holding a newspaper.

"Mom, what's wrong?" KC asked. She hurried over to her.

The president held out the paper so KC and Marshall could see Darla Darling's column. The headline was at least five inches tall. It said:

PRESIDENT MAY
CANCEL WEDDING!

"Someone *is* spying on us!" Lois said, wiping her eyes. "They're hearing our private conversations."

"This has gotten serious," the president said. "No one but us was part of that conversation." He dropped into a chair. "I can't believe someone on my staff is a spy, but if I have to, I'll fire everyone."

"Um, Marsh and I have an idea who it

might be," KC said. She told her mother and the president what Darla Darling had said about her secret caller.

"Someone is giving Darla information over the phone?" Lois said.

"Someone with a scratchy voice!" Marshall went on.

"Yeah, and guess who has a cold?" KC whispered. She pointed to the door through which they'd walked. "Arnold!"

Four pairs of eyes looked at the door.

"Arnold?" the president said. "Well, he is always just outside that door, so he could have overheard, I suppose."

"Someone else knows all your secrets," KC said.

"I'm not sure I want to hear this," the president said. "Okay, who?"

"The vice president," KC whispered.

5
The Truth

"Mary?" the president said. "But she wouldn't . . . I mean, I trust her!"

"Zachary, she *has* seen my dress, and I know we told her where we were going for our honeymoon," KC's mom said.

The president shook his head. "No. I've known Mary for years," he said.

"Could she have told someone without meaning to?" Marshall asked. "Maybe she was just talking, and she accidentally blabbed everything. It happens!"

"I find that hard to believe," Lois said. "I think someone is spying on us. We have to find out who!"

"I have an idea," KC said.

The president rubbed his temples, as if he had a headache. "Tell me. I'll try anything to get to the bottom of this."

KC explained her idea.

"I like it," the president said a minute later. He stood up, crossed the room, and opened his door. "Arnold, may I speak to you in here, please?"

"Yes, sir!" Arnold said with a hoarse voice. He stepped smartly into the room and stood at attention. George the cat followed Arnold inside and flopped on the rug under the president's chair.

"Relax, Arnold," the president said. "I just wanted to tell you something so you're not taken by surprise. Because of all this unwanted publicity, Ms. Corcoran and I have decided to elope. After we're married, we'll just disappear for a short honeymoon."

Arnold's eyes widened, but he didn't say a word.

"Please keep this to yourself, Arnold," the president said. "It's absolutely top-secret! You may go now, and I hope you're taking something for your cold."

"Yes, sir, I am," Arnold said. Then he snapped off a salute, about-faced, and marched out of the room.

"How did I do?" the president asked.

"You did great," Lois said.

"One down, one to go," the president said. He picked up his telephone and pressed a button. "Mary, would you come in for a minute, please?"

The vice president walked into the office through another door. She smiled at

Lois and the kids. "Yes, Mr. President?"

"I have some news about our wedding," the president said.

KC was sitting behind the president. She saw him cross his fingers behind his back.

"I hope this Darla Darling business hasn't made you change your plans," Mary Kincaid said.

"Actually, we *have* made new plans," the president said. "Lois and I are going to elope. We'll be gone for a few days."

Mary Kincaid raised her eyebrows at the news.

"We are the only five who know," the president said. He grinned at his vice president. "And we don't want Darla Darling to be the sixth."

"Of course, sir," Mary Kincaid said. She

closed an imaginary zipper over her lips.

"Fine," the president said. "I'll let you know more as we work out the details."

"Thank you for confiding in me," Mary said. She nodded and left the room. George walked out with the vice president, rubbing against her ankles.

"I feel like a lying skunk," the president said when the door closed.

"Nobody likes to lie," Lois said. "But if this information makes it into Ms. Darling's column, at least we'll know either Arnold or Mary is our spy."

"Yeah," the president grumbled. "My personal guard or my vice president. Great!"

The next morning, still in her slippers, KC took the elevator down to the lobby of her building. She hoped the newspapers had arrived.

They had! A small stack sat on a table outside the elevator doors. KC snatched the top one and jumped back in before the doors closed. She found Darla Darling's column and grinned.

Instead of going back up to her apartment, KC got off on Marshall's floor. She rang his bell as she looked at what Darla had written.

Marshall came to the door barefoot, wearing Spider-Man pajamas.

"Good morning, Spider-Man," KC said. "Read this and get dressed!"

"Can I finish my breakfast first?" Marshall asked.

"Sure, but hurry up, okay?"

Marshall padded to his kitchen with

KC behind him, rattling the newspaper.

Marshall sat and spooned up his cereal. "Is it in there?" he asked, pointing his spoon at the paper.

KC nodded and slid the paper in front of Marshall. There was Darla's smiling face. Beneath her picture a bold headline read:

PRESIDENT AND FIANCÉE
PLAN TO ELOPE!
WATCH MY COLUMN FOR MORE!

"Oh my gosh!" Marshall said. "We were right. It *is* Arnold or Vice President Kincaid! The president is going to flip!"

"That's why you have to hurry up," KC said. "We have to find the snitch before he or she ruins my wedding!"

6
Spying on Spies

Marshall grinned as he slurped up the last spoonful. "*Your* wedding?"

"You know what I mean," KC said. She began pacing back and forth. "We still don't know which one is the spy. We have to catch him or her with the goods."

Marshall put his bowl and spoon in the sink. "What goods?"

"The money, Marshall. Maybe we can catch Arnold or the vice president taking money from Darla."

"KC, we can't follow Arnold. He drives a fast motorcycle, and we don't even know where he lives."

"Okay, but we can spy on the vice president," KC said.

Marshall grinned. "Spying on a spy? I like that."

"Will you get dressed and help?" KC asked. "I don't want Mom to cancel her wedding."

Marshall closed one eye and stared at KC out of the other. "Okay. But promise me we'll go to the park after they're married." He stuck out his pinkie.

KC put out her pinkie. "Promise!" she said. They shook pinkies, and Marshall went to change.

They rushed to the White House and hurried toward the president's private rooms. A marine stood guard at the door, but it wasn't Arnold.

The guard clicked his heels together

when he saw KC and Marshall. "Good morning," he said. "Can I help you?"

"Hi," KC said, surprised to see this short marine instead of tall Arnold. "Have you seen the vice president?"

"No, miss. I just relieved Arnold, and I haven't seen anyone yet but you two." The guard held the door open for them.

In the kitchen, Yvonne was cleaning up. "Good morning. I have a note for you," she told KC. She pulled a folded piece of paper from her uniform pocket.

KC read it out loud to Marshall. *Honey—Zachary and I need some time alone to talk about the wedding. We may be back late. Love, Mom.*

"I left your lunch in the fridge," Yvonne said. "And there's a bowl of fruit on the table."

"Thanks, Yvonne," KC said. "Did they say where they were going?"

"No, miss," Yvonne said. "But I know they took a private car." She hesitated. "They looked pretty unhappy, miss!"

"Um, have you seen the vice president yet this morning?" KC asked.

"No, miss," Yvonne said. She left KC and Marshall in the sunny kitchen. George slipped into the room behind the maid's heels.

As soon as Yvonne was gone, KC grabbed Marshall by the arm. "Now's our chance!" she hissed.

"For what?" he sighed.

"Now's our chance to snoop!" KC said.

"You've been snooping your whole life!" Marshall said. "What's so different today?" He reached for a banana.

"We don't have time to eat," KC said. "If the vice president isn't here yet, we can check out her office!"

"For what?" Marshall said again, dropping the banana.

"I don't know, but if she's selling information to Darla Darling, we might see some evidence," KC said.

The kids walked down the hall toward the vice president's office. A large statue of a Native American family stood next to her door, which was partly open.

KC stuck her nose around the corner and nearly fainted. The vice president was standing with her back to the door, talking on a cell phone.

KC grabbed Marshall, and they both hid behind the statue.

Just then the vice president came

through the door. She walked toward the Oval Office, still talking into her phone.

"I know that," Mary Kincaid was saying. "But this has to be kept secret. . . ."

When she was a few yards away, KC whispered, "Let's try to find out who she's talking to!"

Tiptoeing, they followed the vice president. She passed the Oval Office, still quietly speaking into her phone.

Then she stopped and started to turn around.

Panicking, KC looked for someplace to hide. The closest doorway led to the Oval Office. She knew it would be empty, because the president had left with her mom.

KC poked Marshall, and they both scooted into the Oval Office. There was a

big desk, a few chairs, and a long sofa. A tall plant stood in front of the window.

"This is spooking me out," Marshall whispered. "There has to be a federal law about breaking into the president's office."

"We didn't break in, Marsh," KC said. "Besides, next week, I'll be living in this place."

"Yeah, if we're both not living in jail!" Marshall said.

Suddenly Marshall grabbed KC's hand and yanked her down behind the president's desk.

KC started to protest, but Marshall's hand was across her mouth. She looked at him, trying to figure out what was going on. Marshall's eyes were as big as pancakes.

Then KC understood. She heard footsteps whisper across the carpet. She saw a shadow fall on the wall behind her.

Someone else was checking out the Oval Office!

7

Motorcycle Meeting

KC and Marshall froze behind the desk. They hardly breathed as they heard papers being moved above their heads. Then the shadow moved away.

KC heard the office door open, then close. She crawled from behind the desk and raced for the door.

"What're you doing?" Marshall asked.

"I want to see who that was!" KC hissed. "And what they stole off the president's desk!"

KC slowly eased the door open. She stuck her head out, then back in, like a redheaded turtle.

"It's the vice president!" KC said.

Marshall blinked. "So? She can go into the Oval Office if she wants," he said.

"Come on!" KC said. "Let's follow her."

Walking as quietly as possible, the kids sneaked after the vice president. She left the building and walked toward the employee parking lot. KC and Marshall followed. When she sat on a bench and took out her cell phone, they hid behind some bushes.

"What's she doing?" Marshall asked.

"Talking on her phone again," KC said.

Suddenly they heard a roar. A motorcycle pulled up in front of the bench. When the driver removed his helmet, the kids saw that it was Arnold.

The vice president stood up and slipped her cell phone into her pocket.

From her bag, she took out a small package and handed it to Arnold. They spoke for a minute. Then he put on his helmet and zoomed out of the parking lot. After a few seconds, the vice president hurried back into the building.

"They must both be in on it!" KC said, stepping out from behind the bushes. "Whatever she took off the president's desk, she just gave it to Arnold!"

"And he'll give it to Darla Darling," Marshall said.

KC nodded. "We know it now, but how do we prove it?" she asked.

"I can't prove anything on an empty stomach," Marshall said.

"Okay, come on," KC said. "How can you eat? Don't you feel bad? I really like Arnold and the vice president."

"I like them, too," Marshall said. Then his stomach rumbled.

In the president's kitchen, KC and Marshall sat down at the table. Marshall peeled a banana and started to eat.

George was lying on the counter next to the refrigerator. His bushy tail swept back and forth.

Both kids watched George as he reached for a mouse refrigerator magnet.

The magnet fell to the floor. In a flash, George pounced. He grabbed the mouse in his paws and began chewing on the plastic.

"No, George!" KC said. "Spit it out!" She got down on her knees and moved toward the cat. George jumped up and walked away.

"Now what did you do with that silly

magnet?" KC asked, looking at the floor.

"Maybe it's in his mouth," Marshall said. He slipped behind George and grabbed him.

KC sat on the floor beside Marshall and tried to make George open his mouth.

"Here it is," Marshall said. "It's stuck on his collar."

He pulled the magnet loose and held it out to KC. But she was examining George's collar.

"How could a magnet stick to a plastic collar?" she asked. Slowly, she slid the collar around, studying it closely.

Suddenly KC gasped. She yanked her hands away from the collar as if it were red-hot.

"What?" Marshall asked.

With shaking hands, KC unbuckled George's collar. She opened a drawer, laid the collar inside, and quietly slid the drawer shut. Then she scooted down next to Marshall again.

"KC, are you gonna tell me what's going on?" Marshall asked. "You look all funny."

"That plastic collar has a round metal thing on it," KC whispered. "That's what the magnet was sticking to."

"So? Why do you look so weird?" Marshall asked.

"That piece of metal is a bug," KC said. "A listening device!"

Marshall blinked about seven times. "So . . . someone bugged George? A *cat* is the spy in the White House?"

KC nodded. "George is usually with

the president. That must be how the spy found out all the wedding stuff and reported it to Darla Darling!" she said.

"But who did it?" Marshall asked.

KC shrugged. "It could be anyone who can get close to George," she said. The cat looked at Marshall and meowed.

"So the snitch isn't Arnold or the vice president?" asked Marshall.

"It could still be one of them," KC said. "But I doubt it. They're both here all the time, so why would they have to bug George? But it could be anyone else who works here."

Marshall groaned. "What do we do now? I sure wish the president were here!" he said.

"Well, he's not, but you just gave me a great idea!" KC said. "We can pretend the president is here. And I think I know a way to make the spy come here, too!"

"Am I gonna like this?" Marshall asked, looking worried.

KC beamed. "You're gonna hate it!"

She opened the drawer, lifted out the collar, and carefully placed her hand over the little metal bug. Then she slid next to Marshall. "Just go along with whatever I say," she whispered in his ear.

Marshall gulped, staring at the collar. "You mean we're gonna talk to that thing?"

KC nodded. "Pretend you're in a school play," she said.

"Oh, great," Marshall said. "The last time I was in a play, I got so nervous I nearly puked."

"Well, no puking this time," KC said.

"We have to sound normal. Are you ready?"

Marshall swallowed. "I guess so," he muttered.

KC took her hand off the bug. "Isn't it exciting that Mom and the president are eloping today?" she said with her mouth near the collar.

KC nudged Marshall's foot and placed the collar in his lap.

Marshall's mouth fell open. He stared at the collar as if it were a rattlesnake. He tried to swallow, but his mouth was dry.

KC kicked his foot again. She mouthed the words, *Say something! Someone is listening!*

Marshall took a deep breath before he spoke into the collar. "Yeah, but it's too b-bad they're n-not having their big w-wedding. I was really looking forward to all that c-cake and ice cream."

KC smiled at Marshall and took the collar back. "They have to do it this way to make sure Darla Darling doesn't find out the new honeymoon spot," she said, speaking into the little listening device.

"What time are they eloping?" asked Marshall, taking the collar back. He had stopped stuttering. KC could tell he was getting into it now.

KC glanced up at the kitchen clock. It was almost noon. "Two o'clock," she said, leaning over the collar.

"How are they getting there?" Marshall asked, trying to stop himself from cracking up. "In the president's private plane?"

KC snatched the cat's collar out of Marshall's hands.

"The president doesn't want anyone to recognize him," she said. "He'll be in a taxi and wearing a baseball cap and dark glasses. Mom will have a red scarf over her hair. He's picking her up at the side entrance, near those tall bushes."

Marsh started to giggle, so KC put the collar back in the drawer.

"That was so cool!" Marshall said. "I feel like we're in a James Bond movie!"

"I don't think James Bond giggles," KC said.

"Now what do we do?" Marshall asked.

"We wait till two o'clock," KC said. "And keep our fingers crossed that the spy overheard us and comes to see the president and Mom eloping!"

KC told Marshall the rest of her plan.

Marshall grinned. "I like it," he said.

"Except for one thing. What happens when the spy gets here at two and there's no president and no taxi and no eloping?"

KC looked at him blankly. "Oh," she said. "I didn't think of that."

Marshall sighed. "Good thing James Bond is here to help you." He stood up and reached for the phone. "Here," he said. "Call a taxi."

8

The Fish Takes the Bait!

At ten minutes before two o'clock, KC and Marshall slipped out of the White House. They hid in the bushes near the president's private driveway. KC had her camera.

"What if the spy doesn't show up?" Marshall asked.

"If the spy heard us talking, he or she won't be able to resist!" KC said. "When the president elopes, that's big news! And I'm sure Darla would pay for it."

She looked at her watch. "The taxi should be here any minute. I hope Yvonne is watching."

As if by magic, a taxi slowed and pulled to a stop only a few yards from where KC and Marshall were hiding.

The driver got out and opened the taxi trunk. He was wearing a baseball cap and dark glasses. Following KC's instructions, the driver whistled.

"Get ready," KC mumbled to Marshall.

A woman in a trench coat and red scarf walked briskly out of the side entrance of the White House. She was carrying a small suitcase and wore sunglasses.

"Yvonne looks just like your mother!" Marshall marveled.

"Yeah," KC said, grinning.

Just as Yvonne reached the taxi, KC and Marshall heard a roar. A black motor-cycle zoomed up and screeched to a stop five feet behind the taxi. The person on the bike wore a black leather jacket and pants and a matching helmet. A visor hid the rider's face.

"It's Arnold!" Marshall whispered.

The motorcycle rider straddled the bike. With hands hidden by black leather gloves, he flipped up the visor.

KC saw lipstick and dark curly hair. "No, it's the vice president!" she said.

With the motor still running, the cyclist pulled a small camera from a pocket and snapped a picture of the taxi driver and Yvonne.

KC jumped out of the bushes, her own camera aimed at the motorcycle. "Smile!" she yelled.

The startled rider whipped around and looked at KC. They were only a few feet apart.

KC let out a gasp.

The motorcycle rider wasn't Arnold.

It wasn't the vice president, either.

"Hi, Ms. Darling," KC said.

Darla Darling glared at KC, then flipped down her visor and gunned her engine. With squealing tires, the bike and its rider disappeared into the traffic.

An hour later, the president and KC's mom came back. Yvonne brought them all lemonade in the president's private kitchen. George—without his collar—sat on the president's lap. He purred as his ears were stroked.

"I hope you don't mind me wearing your scarf and sunglasses," Yvonne said to Lois.

"Mind? I think it was a wonderful

idea!" Lois said. "Thank you for your help."

"You're very welcome," Yvonne said, blushing, as she left the room.

"So you told the taxi driver to dress like me, and Yvonne pretended to be your mother," the president said. "And when Darla heard we were eloping today, she shot over here to get the scoop."

KC nodded. "I guess Darla put the bug on George's collar when he got away from us in the rose garden. She must have known that was the only way to bug the White House."

"So it was Darla all the time," KC's mom said. "There was no caller with a scratchy voice. She sat in her office and listened to us talking, then wrote her columns."

"And my own *cat* was the spy!" the president said.

Marshall laughed. "We knew the spy had to be someone near you," he said. "And George is always sitting on your lap."

KC looked at Marshall. "Do you remember when I smelled something minty on George's fur?" she asked. "It was from Darla's mouthwash."

"Mary Kincaid will get quite a chuckle when I tell her you kids thought she might be the motorcycle-riding spy," the president said.

"Do you have to tell her?" KC asked, embarrassed.

"Don't worry," said the president. "She'll be thrilled to know that you kids came to the rescue."

"I wonder what she was giving Arnold in the parking lot?" Marshall asked.

"One way to find out," the president said. He shooed George off his lap and walked over to the door. When he opened the door, Arnold was sipping soup from a mug.

"Arnold, will you step in here, please?"

Arnold came into the room. "Sir?" he said.

The president quickly told Arnold how KC and Marshall had solved the mystery of the White House spy. "But they're wondering what the vice president handed you in the parking lot."

Arnold grinned and held up the soup. "This," he said. "And cough syrup. Ms. Kincaid brings me something every day!"

"What will happen to Darla Darling?"

Marshall asked after Arnold left the room.

"I'm sure the FBI will have a talk with her about the incident," the president said sternly. For a moment, KC felt sorry for Darla. "But no harm done in the long run," the president went on. "We may even invite her to the wedding."

"You *are* getting married!" KC yelled.

"Yes," her mother said. "Saturday at three o'clock. I've decided to wear the green dress, after all. And that night, we'll be in Paris, France!"

9

The Cat Wore White

KC peeked out from behind a tent pole to check out the rose garden. Wooden folding chairs had been set up on the lawn. A long red carpet ran up the aisle.

KC's and her mom's green dresses were the same color as Marshall's vest and the president's bow tie.

A platform had been placed at the back of the garden for the band. They played happy tunes while the guests waited for Lois to walk down the aisle.

At the other end of the red carpet, the president stood by Reverend Murphy, waiting.

"Doesn't the president look nice?" KC whispered to Marshall.

"He looks great, but I feel dorky in this vest," Marshall said.

"I think it's cute," KC said.

"Yeah, right," Marshall said. He held one end of a long green ribbon. The other end was tied to the ring box attached to George's new white collar.

George lay on the carpet, chewing on his ribbon. His tail flipped back and forth. "Please don't run away again," KC begged him.

The wedding ceremony started. Then it was time for KC and Marshall to walk George forward with the rings.

As they marched slowly along the carpet, KC smiled at the vice president, Arnold, and Yvonne.

Darla Darling sat with the other reporters in the press seats. She was busy taking notes. She wasn't even watching the wedding. KC almost giggled, wondering where she parked her motorcycle.

KC stopped at the end of the aisle. Marshall stood next to the president. George rolled over onto his back and stared out at the crowd.

The band started playing the wedding march. KC's mom walked down the aisle in her beautiful dress. Everyone stood and clapped.

When Reverend Murphy nodded, Lois passed her bouquet to KC. Then Marshall opened George's little box and handed the wedding rings to the president.

The couple said, "I do!"

"I now pronounce you husband and

wife!" said Reverend Murphy. The president kissed KC's mom, and everyone cheered.

A few minutes later, the chairs were moved away, and a wooden dance floor was laid over the grass. Waiters brought out food, and the band began playing dance music.

KC watched the president lead her mother onto the dance floor. Once they had begun dancing, all the guests joined in. KC smiled when she saw Arnold dancing with Yvonne.

KC walked up to Marshall. "Do you want to dance?" she asked.

Marshall set his punch cup on a table. He looked into KC's big green eyes.

Then he ran out of the rose garden as fast as his legs would carry him.

Read KC and Marshall's first four adventures!

Who Cloned the President? • Kidnapped at the Capital • The Skeleton in the Smithsonian • A Spy in the White House

Did you know?

Did you know that more than 400 animals have lived in the White House? Most presidents kept pets—horses, dogs, cats, and hamsters. A few had more exotic pets. Thomas Jefferson owned a mockingbird. First Lady Grace Coolidge adored her pet raccoon. President Martin Van Buren had two tiger cubs.

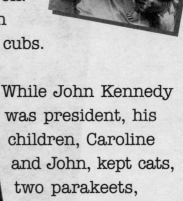

While John Kennedy was president, his children, Caroline and John, kept cats, two parakeets, a canary named Robin, a couple of ponies, and countless hamsters. It is said that some of the

hamsters once climbed into President Kennedy's bathtub!

The president with the most pets was probably Teddy Roosevelt. There was a lion, a hyena, a bunch of bears, even snakes and chickens. And when Teddy's son Archie was sick in bed, his other son Quentin snuck their pony, Algonquin, up the elevator to cheer up Archie in his bedroom!

But the strangest animal to stay in the White House belonged not to a president, but to a Revolutionary War hero. General Lafayette's alligator once slept in the East Room!

A to Z Mysteries®

Help Dink, Josh, and Ruth Rose . . .

. . . solve mysteries from A to Z!

Random House